THIS BLOOMSBURY BOOK

BELONGS TO

....

For Laure, Lilian, Lili and Julio – D.P.
For Rosemary and Parker, a small painter and a big dog – A.M.

First published in Great Britain in 1998 by Bloomsbury Publishing Plc
38 Soho Square, London W1V 5DF
This paperback edition first published 1999

Text copyright © Adrian Mitchell 1998
Illustrations copyright © Daniel Pudles 1998
The moral right of the author and illustrator has been asserted

A CIP catalogue record for this book is available from the British Library
ISBN 0 7475 4188 4 (paperback)
ISBN 0 7475 3555 8 (hardback)

Designed by Dawn Apperley and Suzan Aral
Printed and bound in Belgium by Proost NV, Turnhout

1 3 5 7 9 10 8 6 4 2

Twice my SiZe

Adrian Mitchell and Daniel Pudles

BLOOMSBURY
CHILDREN'S
BOOKS

I've got a friend who's twice my size –

his bright wings flitter and flutter as he flies.

He swoops and he sings most merrily –

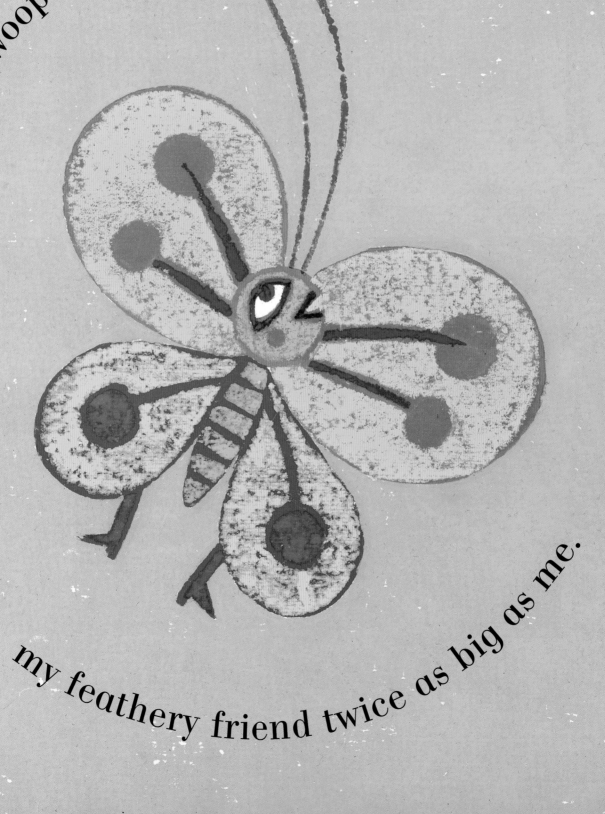

my feathery friend twice as big as me.

We play hide and seek both early and late –

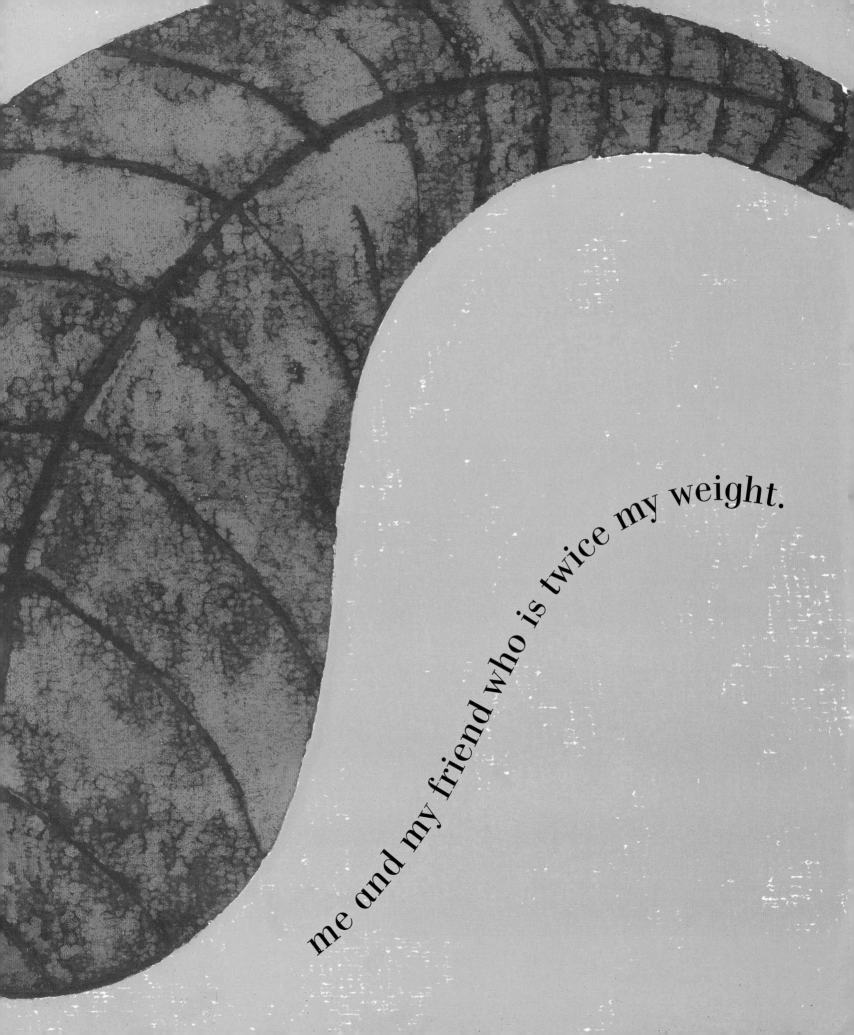

me and my friend who is twice my weight.

We tumble through treetops happily –

for I've got a friend who is twice times me.

He can play rough and tough, but otherwise —

I'm fond of my friend who is twice my size.

To the centre of the earth I'm going to dig –

with my good friend who is twice as big.

Bullies are in for a huge surprise –
for I've got a friend who is twice my size.

I feed him grass, he pulls my barge – me and my

friend who is twice as large.

Over the ice-cream mountains I charge –

to meet my friend who is twice as large.

I gallop down for a seaside swim to meet my friend –

I'm not half as big as him.

I wallow and roll in a summery sea –

for I've got a friend

even bigger than me.

From high in the sky

I smile happily

friends,

on my

all a million times

smaller than me.

Acclaim for this book

'From the tiniest ladybird to the source of the world's light, Mitchell skips through the natural world, doubling the size of friends, abetted by tantalising, bold colour pictures which make you turn the page. *Twice My Size* is a delightful book about friendship and introduces the simple concept of multiplication.'

The Bookseller

'It's fun guessing which animal comes next from the hint on each page. The text is enlivened by unusual woodcut illustrations with an East European feel.'

The Herald